Sept 2015

To - Leah Grace
Happy 4th BirthDAY!
Love,
Auntie Kelly
+
Uncle Denis ♡

The Secret Admirer

To Jennifer Kyle
  — D. W. G.

To Maria, Juliana, and to my Grandmother,
who has never lost her spirit of youth.
                                    — T. S.

Published by Ideals Children's Books
An imprint of Hambleton-Hill Publishing, Inc.
Nashville, Tennessee 37218

Printed and bound in the United States of America

Library of Congress Cataloging-in-Publication Data
Guthrie, Donna.
    The secret admirer / by Donna Guthrie ; illustrated by Tony
Sansevero.
        p.   cm.
    Summary: Since Grams seems to be having trouble meeting her
neighbor Dr. Chadwick, her great-granddaughter decides to play
matchmaker on Valentine's Day.
    ISBN 1-57102-045-4
    [I. Great-grandmothers—Fiction. 2. Old age—Fiction.
3. Valentine's Day—Fiction.] I. Sansevero, Tony, ill. II. Title.
PZ7.G9834Sh   1996
[E]—dc20   95-9985
                                                              CIP
                                                               AC

The illustrations in this book were rendered in colored pencils using live models.
The text type was set in Cochin.
The display type was set in Cochin Italic.
Color separations were made by Color 4, Inc.
Printed and bound by Bertelsmann Corporation.

First Edition

10 9 8 7 6 5 4 3 2 1

The Secret Admirer

By *Donna W. Guthrie*

Illustrated by
Tony Sansevero

Ideals Children's Books • Nashville, Tennessee
an imprint of Hambleton-Hill Publishing, Inc.

Last winter when the ground was covered with snow, my great-grandmother said, "This house is too big for me and the yard is too much work. I think I'll move."

Grams chose an apartment at the Sunny Acres Rest Home and, right before Valentine's Day, Mom and I helped her move in.

Grams put plastic flowers on the window sill and planted seeds in little brown pots to remind her of her garden. She hung a picture of Pop-Pop on the wall along with a picture of me.

"I like my pictures big," said Grams. "My eyes just aren't what they used to be."

I handed her the little wire-rimmed glasses she sometimes wore. But she just smiled and put them in her pocket.

On Saturday morning, Grams and I took the Sunny Acres shopping bus to the grocery store.

As we got on, an old man with fuzzy gray hair stood up and offered us his seat. But Grams just walked on by.

"Grams, there was a seat back there for us," I told her.

"What seat?" said Grams. "I didn't see any seat."

I pointed to her glasses on top of her head. She just laughed and slipped them in her pocket.

On Sunday afternoon, when Grams and I went walking in the
Sunny Acres Park, I pointed out the ducks swimming in the pond.
"What ducks?" said Grams. "I don't see any ducks."

I pointed to her glasses hanging around her neck. She put them on and we watched the ducks paddle away.

Nearby, the old man from the bus was sitting on a bench throwing crumbs to the birds.

"Hello," called Grams. "I'm your new neighbor. I live in apartment 2A, just across the street from you."

The man stared straight ahead at the small birds pecking at his feet. He didn't answer.

"He's not very friendly," said Grams. She put her glasses in her pocket and
we walked on.

On Monday, when Grams and I went to the Sunny Acres Post Office, the old man was waiting outside. He smiled at Grams and tipped his hat.

"Grams," I whispered, "I think that man likes you."

"What man?" she said. "I don't see any man."

I took the glasses from her pocket and handed them to her.

When we came out of the post office, it was cold and the wind was blowing. Grams turned up her collar and called out, "It's a nice day for polar bears, isn't it?"

The old man didn't answer. He just went on reading his mail as if she hadn't spoken.

Grams shook her head sadly. "He's not very friendly," she said.

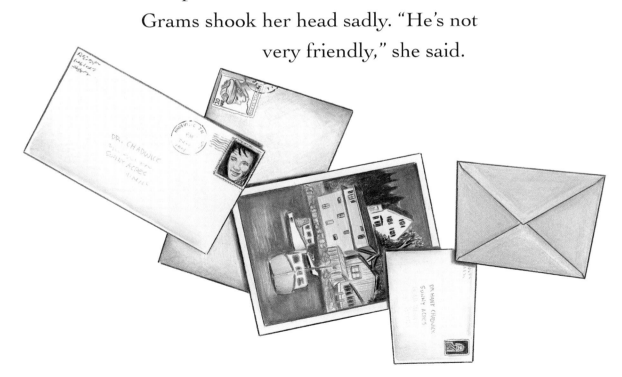

That afternoon Grams and I made cookies. "While the cookies are cooling, let's make some valentines," said Grams. She took out her scissors and some red paper.

"Hearts are the symbol of love," said Grams. She folded the paper in half. "Draw the beginning of the number two on one side, and then cut carefully on the line."

Soon the whole table was filled with red hearts. I made a heart for every person I loved. The extra ones I put on the refrigerator, hung in the window, and pinned in my hair.

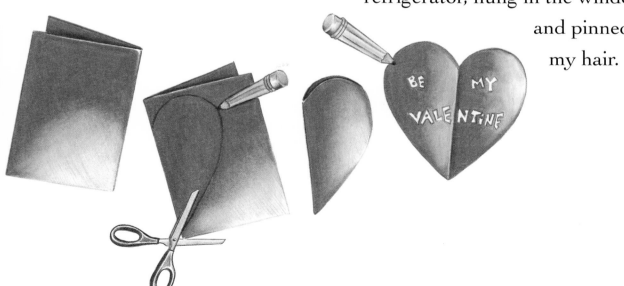

When I left Grams' apartment, the old man was outside
filling up a bird feeder. The wind whirled around us, pulling
at my scarf and making me shiver.

"Hello," he said. "I'm Dr. Chadwick, your great-
grandmother's neighbor. I live in 2B."

I smiled at him. "I like your bird feeder," I said.

"Made it myself. Easy to do — I could teach anybody."

"Would you teach me?" I asked, the wind whistling loudly.

"What's that you say?" Dr. Chadwick touched his
ear. "You have to speak up. I don't hear as well as I
used to — especially when I forget to
wear my hearing aid."

The thick, gray clouds overhead gathered above us and the wind blew harder. Dr. Chadwick buttoned up his coat. "It's a nice day for polar bears, isn't it?"

"That's what Grams always says."

"Not to me," said Dr. Chadwick. "Every time I smile or tip my hat, she walks on by as if she doesn't even see me. She's not very friendly."

Just then Grams came to her window and looked out. We both waved, but she didn't wave back. She wasn't wearing her glasses.

"See what I mean?" said Dr. Chadwick. He went back to filling his bird feeder.

That night I took some red paper and made two big hearts. On each one I wrote a secret message. I hid them in my bottom drawer and waited for Valentine's Day.

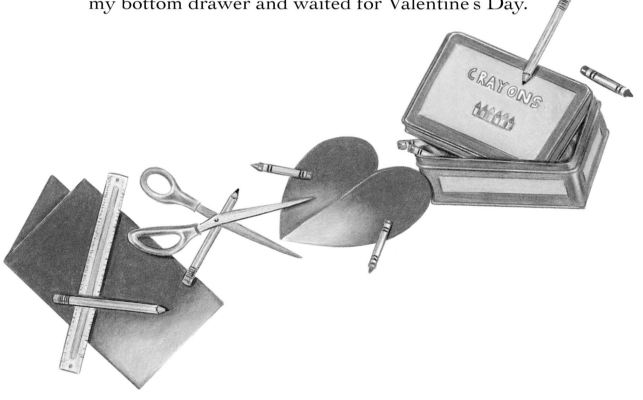

On Valentine's Day I got up very early. Snow had fallen during the night. I put on my winter boots, my heavy coat, and the valentine mittens from Grams. Walking through the deep, wet snow to the Sunny Acres Rest Home, I was very quiet. Everyone was still resting.

I tiptoed up to apartment 2A and slipped a valentine under Grams'
door. Silently I crept across the street to Dr. Chadwick's building and
slipped a valentine under his door too. Then I hurried away.

That afternoon when I stopped by to visit, Grams said, "Look at the valentine I received today. It's from a secret admirer."

"A secret admirer?" I tried not to giggle. "I wonder who that could be?"

"Oh, I think I know," said Grams. She put on her glasses and went to the window.

Down below, Dr. Chadwick was shoveling the snow from his sidewalk. Grams opened the window and waved.

Dr. Chadwick tipped his hat.

"It's a nice day, isn't it?" called Grams.

"Only for polar bears," replied Dr. Chadwick.

Grams laughed. "Why don't you come up for tea?"

"I'd like that," said Dr. Chadwick. "I'll be right in, as soon as I finish this."

For the rest of the afternoon, Dr. Chadwick and I sat in Grams' kitchen drinking tea and eating valentine cookies. While they talked, I drew plans for my bird feeder.

Finally, when it was time to go, Dr. Chadwick stood up and said, "Thank you for the tea." Then he added with a smile, "And I can't remember the last time someone sent me a valentine."

Grams winked at me. "You're very welcome," she said. "I hope I'll 'see' you soon."

"Of course," said Dr. Chadwick, "and I'll keep an 'ear' open for you."

They both laughed.

When Dr. Chadwick left, I admitted what I had done. "This morning I sent Dr. Chadwick a valentine asking him to wear his hearing aid. That way he could hear you when you spoke to him."

"I know," said Grams.

"And I sent a valentine to you asking you to wear your eyeglasses. So you could see him when he tips his hat."

"I know," she said.

"I'm sorry, Grams, but you don't really have a secret admirer."

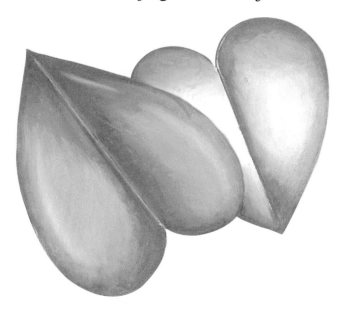

Grams looked out the window and smiled,

"Oh, I wouldn't be so sure about that!"